Covered by the Blood

An African-American Family's
Journey from Slavery

A PERSONAL STORY

Covered by the Blood

An African-American Family's Journey from Slavery

A PERSONAL STORY

Elvie L. Barlow Sr.

ISBN: 978-1-4276-5239-3

Cover photography provided by the Barlow Family Archives

Dedication

I will first give honor to my Lord and Savior, Jesus Christ. Without Him this book would not be written. Who said in His holy word, I can do all things through him, who strengthens me.

I would like to dedicate this book to my great, great, great, great, grandmother, who through her life preserved her dignity. I would also like to dedicate this book to my children: Tynesa, Catherine, Elvie Jr., Michael, Abigail; and, to all my nieces and nephews.

I love you all.

Elvie

Contents

Preface

What if you were all alone in an unfamiliar place? Or if there were no light when night fell? That feeling would be so lonely and empty that your mind could not withstand or comprehend the circumstances that you are in. Sometimes we find ourselves in lonely places with no one to talk to or understand the lonely, empty situations we are in. And with that there is an element of fear suddenly thrust upon us. If this lonely feeling persists, it will overtake and consume us. It may even send us into a state of depression. I believe my ancestors found themselves in a lonely state of mind and spirit, beginning as early as their captivity as slaves in Africa.

They were sold. Some were stolen from homes where the comforts of a mother and father were never realized again. And they realized they would never see their loved ones again they would miss the nurturing and the love that only a mother, father or loved one could give. They were left devastated and yes, very alone. The tear left everlasting emotional and spiritual damage. A truly traumatic experience it remains.

In "normal" situations, this would be a recipe for disaster. All hope is gone and the enemy has won. Future hopes and dreams would be lost forever. But this book tells the story of the "other normal" and how situations in life sometimes usher in another dimension, the spiritual dimension.

The spiritual dimension is the state that determines our future and allows our hopes and dreams to be realized. It is the spiritual state that made a difference in the lives of my ancestors and the lives of the millions who made the journey to America in bondage. It is the spiritual dimension that gives each of us an inner strength and peace of mind.

My people were strong and persistent. They, like many others, survived and thrived in America under the most difficult circumstances.

I can only imagine the thoughts that these people had as they were torn away from their families, friends and all things familiar to face the journey from Africa to hell on Earth. Many didn't make it. They were thrown overboard because they were dead or too sick, or they would jump to their deaths because they were tired of the journey. And, if by chance they survived the journey, to America, Europe, Caribbean, Brazil or other places they were sold and carted off like herds of animals bound in irons and chains to plantations. There they would work their entire lives as servants, field hands and Lord only knows what else. The main purpose for the Africans was to work for the benefit of their "owners."

I made a point to visit several slave auction sites that still exist between Charleston and Memphis . A chill ran through my body when I imagined the fear and uncertainty these people must have felt. To image the callous arrogance of people who bought other people frightened me...

Nevertheless, for others (such as the slave owners or "masters"), despite all the suffering and inhumanity of slavery, it was a time enjoyed. They truly benefited from all that America had to offer. It was a time in America when anyone, other than black people, could come to America and realize the riches of this country. It didn't matter if you came to America dirt poor, there were vast opportunities to gain great wealth .

The business of Slavery was huge and very instrumental to the making of the Americans and the United States we know today. It is accurate to state that America was built on the backs of African Slaves. Of all the industries present in America during the slave period, the slave trade was number one, larger than the railroad and the cotton industries combined.

This book describes an incredible love. This love has not only been manifest in my life but in the lives of those who journeyed to America in chains, my ancestors as far back as the 1700s. This love is a spiritual love manifesting itself as a soft, sweet, and warm embrace of the spirit of God. Through this love my family, descended from slaves in America, accomplished greatness in spite of adversity. This book is a remarkable story of men and women who decided not to be victims, though they were victimized, and through hard work, struggle, sacrifice, and courage they too acquired wealth in America even though they were enslaved and African.

Elvie Barlow Sr.

Introduction

The story contained in Covered by the Blood takes the reader on a journey and show the connectivity and continuity of the African Spirit in America. It is a story about the Stephens family from Dougherty County in Albany, Georgia. Through exhaustive research of genealogical and financial records actual documents were uncovered in what was a virtual tomb... a grandmother's lockbox. Discover the long preserved treasures of great, great, great, grandfather Titus Stephens, Sr. through letters, deeds of trust, poetry and other narratives that reveal the rarely discussed fact that some African-Americans owned and inherited property during the slavery period in America. Perhaps most remarkable, the property that was negotiated and purchased by the enslaved ancestor was held on to and cherished by family members throughout the years, and even through today.

It is widely known how so-called "slaves" were depicted as powerless, dimwitted, disrespected, manipulated, whipped, frightened and disenfranchised people of African descent. That they were subjected to hedonistic acts by a cruel, intolerant and sadistic people referred to as "masters." Though historical evidence proves this, it is also true that there were those who were the antithesis of the portrayal.

For the purposes of this book, we refer to those who defied tradition as "Cushites." They were Africans who in spite of obstacles including hard times and persecutions were spirit-driven, self-determined, strategic and economically astute people with vision and purpose for their future. The Cushites were inventive entrepreneurs who devised plans that proved beneficial for them and for the generations that followed.

To envision a Cushite, one need only think of Harriet Tubman, Cinque, Ida B. Wells, Fredrick Douglas, Moses, Malcolm X, Fannie Lou Hamer and Ella Baker who exemplified the spirit of determination by persevering through the pains of torture, humiliation and disrespect to become "free"… by any means necessary!

That is the quality that makes men, men; women, women; and leaders, leaders. This trait is not as rare in that era as portrayers of history depict it to be. "Covered by the Blood" is a book that not only reveals this as an observed and documented fact, it reveals that it is a the product of good ole "home-training."

Readers will also begin to understand ancient mysteries and disciplines of African traditions and Biblical studies — the quality, trait, and characteristics of the Cushites are fighting revolutionary spirits with an instilled power of refusal to succumb to the temptation of surrender despite oppression and abuse. These are people "Covered by the Blood."

This is the story of those noteworthy traits. And what a notable journey it is.

C. Sade Turnipseed

My Discovery

About twenty years ago, when going through papers that belonged to my grandmother, I discovered a document that stood out. I now wonder if my grandmother had deliberately left these papers in an attempt to bring it to my attention. She had been going through the early stage of Alzheimer's when I found them. All I can be sure of is that those papers were her prized possession.

My grandmother, I remembered at the time, had gone through those papers time and time again. It happened on a regular basis during my younger years.

But looking through them twenty years ago, there just seemed to be something different about one of the documents. It wasn't just old, it was odd looking and it seemed to speak to me. But, I didn't listen. I was too busy trying to keep up with my grandmother and the effects of an illness that affects so many elderly. My grandmother would wander. She often rummaged through papers or whatever she could get her hands on. Most of the time, she would lose or destroy things she handled. There was something about this one piece of paper that spoke to my soul asking me to retrieve it for safekeeping. So, I just picked up and stored it away. It was about thirteen years later when I discovered this document again.

As my grandmother did, I sat down one day and began to rummage through old papers, not because of Alzheimer's, I hope. But, there again was that document I put away many years before. I read it. I realized this was a living, breathing document with a whole lot to tell me. Little did I know, this document revealed the history of a people whose stories had not yet been told. It had been sleeping, waiting to be awakened by someone who would tell story of determination, encouragement, hatred and love. The document was so powerful that it could even change and transform my own life.

I also discovered something very spiritual about the story that the document revealed. It has an important link to a biblical story about the people of Ethiopia called "Cushites."

The Cushites today are called the "Ethiopian Jews." The late Dr. George McCalep, pastor of Green Forest Baptist Church, in Decatur, Georgia delivered a sermon about the Ethiopian Jews, or Cushites. At the height of their reign, they ruled the world and were feared by all nations. I was not surprised by the words of the sermon, just enlightened. This was the first time in a long time that a minister talked about a subject like this.

The sermon was inspirational and very educational. I had always wondered, even as a child, why black people didn't seem to have a place in history in the school books or in Sunday school lessons. And why we were so hated in the United States, specifically in South Georgia where I was born and raised.

I remembered the Civil Rights Movement in the United States, during the '50s and '60s. As a young man I compared it to apartheid of South Africa. There was never an occasion that made African Americans feel proud. I like many African Americans wanted to be a proud of myself and of my people, and was constantly looking for something or someone to take pride in. I believe those of us who lived through the '50s, '60s, and even the '70s, struggled to come out of that era with dignity and some degree of sanity. We were on a mission to feel as though we were living productive and useful lives. The problem was it was difficult to find anything substantive to cling to.

Though there was no information about Black history widely circulated, during the Civil Rights Movement. We did have James Brown, who inspired us all with songs like "Say it Loud--I'm Black and I'm Proud," "I Don't Want Nobody to Give Me Nothing (Open the Door, I'll Get it Myself)," and others. Through those songs, I saw myself in a different light. It was finally all right to be "Black and Proud."

Back to the sermon that Sunday morning, the thing that most prominently stuck out was Dr. McCalep's research of the Bible and how he interpreted Black history. He explained that black men were misrepresented in the Bible. I had always felt the same way. He focused on the Bible passage:

"In that time shall the present be brought unto the Lord of hosts of a people scattered and peeled, and from a people terrible from their beginning hitherto; a nation meted out and trodden under foot, whose land the rivers have spoiled, the place of the name of the LORD of hosts, the mount Zion (Isaiah 18:7)."

This passage, though troubling, is not so surprising. Whenever things just didn't seem right, my grandmother would always say, "There's something in the milk that's not clean," and "There's a dead cat on the line somewhere."

The Sunday sermon message eased my mind. I began to realize why there was such an assertive effort to hate, kill, and suppress African American people. The Spirit of the Lord made it apparent to me, in a clear message that my people are great.

According to the Bible, Ham had four sons (Gen. 10:6) Kush, Miriam, Put, and Canaan. Kush was the father of the Ethiopian people. Kush is the Hebrew word for "black." Ethiopia is a Greek word meaning "black face."

Not to re-preach the sermon but I want the reader of this book to connect the Biblical stories to the members of my family. It is important to understand the connection with the history of my ancestors.

Having taught Sunday School for over 30 years, I have a deep and abiding faith in scripture. I have learned to listen to the Word. So from Dr. McCalep's sermon, I took away a deep appreciation. It was the Egyptian (Black woman) sons that inherited the promise of God and passed on the birthright (Gen. 48:14-16).

The name "Israel" was passed on to two African men. And God said, "Let them grow." Who was God referring to as "them?" They were African men of Egypt, who became the Children of Israel. What a powerful Biblical story.

I can never forget that the greatest statue of the world stands in Egypt, the "Sphinx." This statue shows that ancient Egyptians were black people. These were the people who created religion, science, engineering, and writing. The first to practice medicine, architecture, astronomy, agriculture, and they created the first banking system. I came to realize that the same God who was watching over the Ancient Ethiopians and Egyptians was watching over my ancestors.

Looking back, I always believed that black people were powerful rulers in history. I just needed to realize that the history of this people is more than what we are taught in school.

Little did I know, I would discover a rich and proud history in my family's old and nearly discarded documents. There was the link. I am now determined, more so than ever before, to continually uncover as much as I can about my ancestors by writing this and other books. I will tell the true story of my biblical and African heritage.

The Voyage

John Mock was born in Germany. He along with thousands of other immigrants from Europe arrived at Ellis Island in 1844. Only a few months after landing on the Eastern shore he arrived in Albany, Georgia. The reasons why he left Germany, we will never know. However, I would venture a guess that he was not stripped from his family and native land and forced to come to America and work for no pay. He also most certainly didn't travel in the bottom of a slave ship. And, upon arrival in America, he most certainly was not sold to the highest bidder. Instead, he was presented with opportunities to travel and look forward to all the benefits this new frontier had to offer. America was the land of opportunities for folks like John Mock who came seeking a chance at a better life.

Mock brought with him a wife and two children. When they arrived in Albany, they settled in east Dougherty County. It took a relatively short period of time for him to amass a huge amount of property, thereby affording him the opportunity to place his family in Albany's upper echelon.

This remarkable success story is shared and enjoyed by the Mock family and many other immigrants like them. I believe historians marvel at how within only a few years, so many people achieved wealth in this country, a country not native to them. I find it interesting to contrast my ancestors' voyage to the work ethic in America. I'd say it is a night and day difference.

One group of people freely left their native land in search of better opportunities for themselves; the other was forced from their native land to ensure a better life for others. One group traveled on deck of the ship; the other in chains in the bowels. One group, upon arrival in America was filled with joy and excitement; the other was faced with a life filled with misery, pain, sadness, uncertainty and despair.

This is not just a tale of two families with diametrically opposing outlooks regarding their journey to and experiences in America. It is the story of how the American society has historically ensured the success of many hard-working people; while at the same time others' futures were not insured.

Our Journey Begins...

Remembering the Enemy -
The Willie Lynch Letter

There has never been a more evil institution than slavery. One of the manifestations of the institutionalization is the "Willie Lynch Speech."

Willie Lynch was a slave owner, who devised a plan to help keep Black people divided. This is the infamous statement of Willie Lynch...

Gentlemen:

I greet you here on the banks of the James River in the year of our lord, one thousand seven hundred and twelve. First, I shall thank you, the gentlemen of the colony of Virginia, for bringing me here. I am here to help you solve some of your problems with slaves. Your invitation reached me in my modest plantation in the West Indies where I have experimented with some of the newest and oldest methods for control of slaves. Ancient Rome would envy us if my program were implemented. As our boat sailed south on the James River, named for our illustrious King James, whose Bible we Cherish, I saw enough to know that our problem is not unique. While Rome used cords or wood as crosses for standing human bodies along the old highways in great numbers, you are here using the tree and the rope on occasion. I caught the whiff of a dead slave hanging from a tree a couple of miles back. You are losing valuable stock by hangings. You are having uprisings. Slaves are running away, your crops are sometimes left in the fields too long for maximum profit, you suffer occasional fires, your animals are killed. Gentleman,.. you know what your problems are I do not need to elaborate. I am not here to enumerate your problems. I am here to introduce you to a method of solving them.

In my bag, I have a foolproof method for controlling your slaves. I guarantee every one of you that if installed it will control the slaves for at least three hundred years. My method is simple, any member of your family or any OVERSEER can use it.

I have outlined a number of differences among the slaves, and I take these differences and make them bigger. I use FEAR, DISTRUST, and ENVY for control purposes. These methods have worked on my modest plantation in the West Indies, and it will work throughout the SOUTH. Take this simple little list of differences and think about them. On the top of my list is "AGE" but it is only there because it starts with an "A"; The second is "COLOR" or shade; there is INTELLIGENCE, SIZE, SEX, SIZE OF PLANTATION, ATTITUDE of owner, whether the slaves live in the valley, on a hill, east or west, north, south, have fine or coarse hair, or are tall or short. Now that you have a list of differences, I shall give you an outline of action--but before that, I shall assure *you that DISTRUST IS STRONGER THAN TRUST, AND ENVY IS STRONGER THAN ADULATION, RESPECT OR ADMIRATION.*

The black slave, after receiving this indoctrination, shall carry on and will become self-refueling and self-generating for hundreds of years, maybe thousands.

Don't forget you must pitch the old black vs. the young black males, and the young black male against the old black male. You must use the dark skinned slaves vs. the light skin slaves. You must use the female vs. the male, and the male vs. the female. You must always have your servants and OVERSEERS distrust all blacks, but it is necessary that your slaves trust and depend on us.

Gentlemen, these kits are your keys to control, use them. Never miss an opportunity. My plan is guaranteed, and the good thing about this plan is that if used intensely for one year the slave will remain perpetually distrustful.

-William Lynch-1772

This systemized way of producing and governing African people gives a snap shot into the mindset of some white slave owners and how, during that period of time they viewed slavery and African people. It also gives us a historical perspective of what the enslaved, such as my grandparents, had to contend with, living during the time of Willie Lynch.

The Willie Lynch letter is about control, power, hatred and fear, which tainted the thinking of people, black and white, for centuries. I would further suggest that the impact of that statement is felt today. It was essential for some white slave owners to feel as though they were in complete control and that included the maintaining the powerful influences they held over the culture and destiny of the African people.

I have internalized the impact of the Willie Lynch statement. The method he laid out was a formula to control people like my great, great, great, great, grandparents and me. It became the white slave owner's method for implementing complete control over the enslaved by dividing and conquering, making people aware of differences in each other, and by celebrating the discord, or punishing the strong and rewarding the weak. This method or formula ,negative reinforcement, has been so firmly implanted that it is now promoted as the natural instinct of African people.

This is so fundamentally wrong, on so many levels, that anyone who believes this about me or my people are pathological and in need of spiritual healing and God's intervention. To have the desire to control everything in another person's life: that's pathetic. And we have to remember there is a God. And God don't like the ugly ways people are treated. This is what we are still faced with today. Just look around you. Or, if you are so privileged, look outside of your environment. You will see the residuals of the Willie Lynch method of thinking, wanting to be in control of other people's destiny, still today.

It is said, "Absolute power corrupts absolutely."

The Willie Lynch speech presents a picture of mental slavery, which is still institutionalized and discernable in most aspects of our lives in America. However, in all fairness, I must point out that neither Willie Lynch's words, nor his methods negatively influenced all white slave owners during that time period. Some were strong enough to resist the temptation of total and complete control. And that applies to the strength of the enslaved as well. Some were strong enough to resist the attempts to manipulate their thinking with the implementation of this particular mind control technique.

My Great, Great, Great, Great, Grandmother Lydia Stephens

The journey into the bowels of my personal history took me to the late 1700s in Charleston, South Carolina. During this period, Charleston was a rural agricultural area with rice, as the main crop. The rice plantations stretched around Charleston like a horseshoe with the sea at its opening. It was a beautiful, lush city. More importantly, it was the city where most of the Slave ships docked with their precious cargo of enslaved Africans. From what I've learned about my family's crossing over the Middle Passage, from Africa into America, Charleston is the place that held the records of my great, great, great, great grandparents.

Slave Quarters

Once all the information I was gathering began to resonate within me, I realized with certainty that the City of Charleston held the key to my discoveries. It was there where the suffering from hardships was documented for at least one of my ancestors. (Of course, this was not the first place of such pain. That began in Africa, the land of the Cushites, when they were captured by foreigners and treated inhumanely.)

For the purpose of this book, it is important to continually emphasize that the Cushites were a powerful people, whose spirit still resonates with us today.

From what my grandparents told me, my great, great, great, great grandmother named Lydia was born somewhere on the West Coast of Africa. She crossed the Middle Passage in chains and was sold on the auction block in Charleston, to the household of John Stephens, in 1790.

It was there that she labored for the Stephens family, sometimes in the fields and other times as the housekeeper, while all the time missing her native land, family and loved ones. Her life was one of servitude to her so-called master. She like all other enslaved people washed her master's clothes, cooked their food, cleaned their houses and were hired out to work in the sugar cane and rice fields around Charleston.

That's all I was able to gather on Lydia Stephens. However…

My Great Great Great Grandfather Titus Stephens, Sr.

At this point in my journey of discovery, my primary source of research was the 1810 census. The rest, I recalled from what my great grandmother, grandmother and mother passed along to me.

From the time I was little, through to my teenage years, my great grandmother told me wonderful stories of our ancestors coming to this country from Africa. Most of the time, I would be sitting on a five-gallon oil can, by the old-wood-burning stove trying to keep warm during the winter months, while my great grandmother cooked dinner, or canned peas and butter beans in Mason jars. I had to earn the right to be there. My job was to keep the fire burning in the stove. I listened intently to engaging conversation among the elders. According to my empirical research and recollection there was not a long lineage of enslavement, particularly mental enslavement.

Titus, Stephens Sr. married Darcus. She too had been physically, but not mentally enslaved. The couple had four children. Their names were: Titus Stephens Jr., Anna Paxton, Clarisy Crawford, and Lydia Stephens (my great, great, Grandmother). I am not sure why Anna and Clarisy have different last names. It could be that Darcus had two children before she married Ttus Sr. There were not many records on them that I could find to determine whether they were ever freed from physical enslavement. I do know my great, great, uncle Titus Stephens Jr. was born in 1858 and my great, great, grandmother Lydia was born in 1862 before the Emancipation Proclamation.

Now here is where our journey begins to get very interesting…

The City of Charleston was the place where my great, great, great, great, grandmother, Lydia, a stunningly beautiful Cushite woman, had been repeatedly sexually abused and molested by her so-called "master." These countless rapes ultimately resulted in the birth of a male child. That child was my great, great, great, grandfather Titus Stephens Sr.

The name given to Titus is significant, because it has both biblical and historical meanings. In the bible the term, Titus, was a companion of Saint Paul and received one of Paul's epistles in the Bible. Historically, the Latin root word of Titus is titulus meaning "title of honor."

Titus lived with his mother and his "master" father, until he was nine years old. At the age of nine, he was sold off by his biological father, and taken away from his mother. That is how my family got to the southwest Georgia region.

Southern Mansion

One thing about all this still remains a problem for me. You got it. How is it possible, on God's Earth, for a man to sell his own son?

I discovered one possible reason when I visited the Slave Haven Underground Railroad Museum in Memphis, Tennessee. While there, the tour guide told many stories about the selling of slaves. One story was about how uncomfortable it was for slave owners, who fathered children by enslaved women, to be continually reminded of his atrocious behaviors, by the mere presence of the child, day after day, year after year.

In the mind of enslavers, they "owned" their slaves. Therefore, they made their own children commodities and that guilt was too heavy to carry around every day. So, they didn't. To this point, my forefather (the enslaver) was incapable of dealing with the dilemma like a man. Therefore, his best option was to remove the constant reminder of hisact of molestation by selling his offspring. Hence, my great, great, great,　grandfather Titus had to be removed from his mother and the situation.

I am sure his mother Lydia was filled with grief. I am certain it was probably too much to bear. We can only pray that she realized her son was in God's hands and that God's plan was to bless him and his seed for generations to come. The love between Titus and his mom was passed down from generation to generation. Though they never saw each other again, this was not the end of the Titus and Lydia story.

I believe in destiny. There is no question that the lives of each of my family members would have been very different if my great, great, great,　grandfather Titus Sr., had not been bought and sold by the highest bidder, who brought him to southern Georgia.

The bright side was that there was land and people waiting to help him break the chain of slavery, which had a strangle hold on most African people in America. This was the beginning of a series of events that I am proud to say continues to this day. A new dawn was on the horizon. I often asked those in the family older than me, "How was it that this young man, this Cushite, overcame Willie Lynch's strategy for control?"

This is one of the answers I received...

By the time Titus was sold in 1819, the institution of slavery was deeply entrenched in America. There had to have been a greater force than himself at work to overcome the strategic methods and policies of Willie Lynch and his disciples. That greater force was our spiritual beliefs and our African heritage.

Fortunately, Titus landed on a plantation whereby his slaver did not follow the Willie Lynch doctrine to manage and control their enslaved. My family believes his mother Lydia had some "spiritual" thing to do with that.

J.W. Mock was his name. He, to his credit, did not follow the racist and torturous norm of the slave era. Instead, from what was revealed to me, he seemed to have a rather unnatural respect and admiration for my relatives, while still holding on to his stake in the institution of slavery.

Without a doubt, it was the institution of slavery that built and sustained America. We can never forget the misery of humans whose lives were lost, torn and beaten down by the shackles of slavery. And, until we come to grips with the impact slavery had on America, we will never move in a direction that is healthy for all.

Even during one of the most troubling periods in American history, the Civil War, which claimed over 500,000 lives, Titus Stephens did not abandon the south. I believe he knew he was blessed and highly favored and that the Lord was covering him with his protective spirit, the warm embrace of Lydia.

It has been over two hundred years and many Americans are still indoctrinated by the prescription for the destruction of the African mind. However, my ancestor Titus Stephens was one that, let it be known, he was more than property. He could have been a submissive slave who submitted to the system. Or a radical slave revolting and running away to the freedom of the north. But he didn't. He stood, determined to be treated as a human being, a man who loved his family. He like many others deserved to be treated with the respect and honor of any hard-working person. J.W. Mock respected Mr. Titus Stephens.

One of the main reasons Titus was transported from Charleston to Albany, Dougherty County, Georgia was because he was needed to work on the plantations. Before the Civil War, Albany was becoming the "Egypt of America." According to W. E. B. Dubose, just prior to the Civil War Albany, Georgia was great cotton country. The soil was dark and fertile and the production of cotton was the landowner's key to wealth.

"Then came the black slaves. Day after day the clank of chained feet marching from Virginia and Carolina to Georgia was heard in these rich swamplands. Day after day the songs of the callous, the wail of the motherless, and the muttered curses of the wretched echoed from the Flint to the Chickasawhatchee, until by 1860 there had risen in West Dougherty perhaps the richest slave kingdom the modern world ever knew. A hundred and fifty barons commanded the labor of nearly six thousand Negroes, held sway over farms with ninety thousand acres of tilled land, valued even in times of cheap soil at three millions of dollars. Twenty thousand bales of ginned cotton went yearly to England, New and Old; and men that came

there bankrupt made money and grew rich. In a single decade the cotton output increased four-fold and the value of lands was tripled."

"The Souls of Black Folk" 1903,
W.E.B. Du Bois (1868–1963)

I must admit J.W. Mock played a critical role in my family's destiny by allowing Grandfather Titus to acquire land, before the War began. And, this is the land my family still owns today.

J. W. Mock understood the business of the slave trade and capitalized on it. He realized that to build his fortune and this country he needed free slave labor. He owned a great plantation in Dougherty County, Georgia and needed the fields of this vast plantation to be plowed. With his plantation and acquired wealth, he obtained notoriety. He was well known and respected as a successful planter during the slavery era. His family's prominent status is still honored. As a matter of fact, there is a road in Albany, Georgia named in honor of the Mock family. I do wonder why J. W. Mock allowed Titus to acquire the land. Was it some kind of negotiation or some kind of work-for-pay system? No one seems to be able to tell me this for certain.

My first thought, and what I would like to believe, is that Titus worked so hard and was so faithful that after a period of time, Mock willed him the land on his deathbed. I have no proof of this. But I would just like to give Mock the benefit of doubt and assume him to be humane in this instance. That now sheds a different light on the rules laid out in Willie Lynch's speech and on the perception we have about what is possible in America. I would like to believe that, in some (rare) instances, the enslaved Africans were treated somewhat fairly and humanely by their enslavers.

However, can you imagine your employer, say a farmer in Mississippi, giving an employee one hundred (100) acres of prime land today?

Neither can I.

But, we can project hope and present the case of my family as a healthy alternative to the way people treat each other.

My second thought follows the tradition of slavery, as history teaches us. No one gave Blacks anything. However, on occasion these so-called masters did allow the enslaved to earn money (credit) after working their normal workday. In many cases, a sizeable percentage of that money earned by the slave would have to be given to the slave master. If my great, great, great, grandfather purchased the farmland, he would have had to work on the plantation during the day and work his farm, or a neighboring farm at night. Whatever it took, two things are clear. It was the purpose and the promise of the good Lord the Almighty God. And Miss Lydia!

As the owner of property, in Albany, Dougherty County, Georgia in the 1860s, Titus was not allowed to show a profit at the harvest of his crops and he was not allowed to process cotton, or any other lucrative business. No matter what the situation Blacks were not allowed to earn more than whites.

The Dougherty County 1870 Tax Book states "African-Americans were not landowners in 1870." But, we know for a fact that African- Americans were landowners. It was a common practice for land to be held in the name of white patrons. This was the case with J. W. Mock and Titus Stephens. The land acquired by Titus was probably after the passing of J.W. Mock, but before the Civil War. This situation is not uncommon since during the 1860s, this arrangement provided protection for both parties.

Titus's role and responsibilities while enslaved were undeniably to J.W. Mock. This is what brought him the protection he needed from whites that did not like the idea of Titus, or any Black person, owning land. This fact was realized when I could find no evidence that showed any attempt (throughout the years) to destroy our property. Perhaps, the land acquisition was a secret. I can only speculate on this because there is only the physical deed, which does not show any actual financial transaction. All we know for sure is that it did happen, somehow, someway.

There was something very different about this master/slave relationship. Growing up in the south, I remembered how the evil system of "Jim Crow" aided and abetted the mind-control mandate. Jim Crow was the contemporary of the Willie Lynch system of control and power. What it was supposed to do is teach us "our place." Jim Crow, just like Willie Lynch, was very effective.

However, the character and strength displayed by my grandfather, Titus makes my family proud. He lived to become the man God made him to be and the man his mother Lydia prepared him to become during those nine years in Charleston.

There were so many things his mother must have told him. As the story goes, she taught him tools of survival, the things he had to remember and adhere to for the rest of his life.

These are a few lessons that have been passed down to me and to my children:

- Never give up on anything.

- No matter what situation you are in, you can overcome.

- Never forget that you are covered by the blood of Jesus Christ and all the African ancestors, who died crossing the Middle Passage going into enslavement around the world.

Another one of those very important lessons was the instruction on investing in our legacy for future generations. It was not about just working on behalf of the master. Having a "get a job" mentality is how and why "Jim Crow" was so effective. Those without these lessons were those who never knew how to reach their full potential. Titus had to be very spiritual and wise in his dealing. Even though he was allowed to acquire land and farm it, he was still a slave. There were shackles on his ability to reach full potential. Those shackles deterred him from competing against the economic society at that time.

Ultimately, what my great, great, great, grandfather left us, as a birthright was his dignity. Titus, like any man, wanted something to call his own. He wanted wealth not just money. He understood that money is what you use to buy goods and services. But wealth is what passes on to future generations. This man's amazing strength and courage has benefited his family and serves as a beacon of light for anyone who dares to dream the impossible.

With this as Titus's directive and preparation, he bought land; tilled his own soil and raised his family with dignity. I am so grateful for God and his mom. It is written, "A good father leaves a legacy for his family." The Cushites knew their struggle was not about them alone, but it was also about struggle for those to come.

My struggles in life have made me appreciate my forefathers even more greatly. They were trailblazers. The leadership trait of Titus was emulated by his daughter Lydia; and granddaughter, my great grandmother Clemmie Russell Holmes; and, her daughter my grandmother Rubye Sullivan. Their lives were not wasted. They stood for their principles and made a way for themselves. I continue to pray to God that I can to display that kind, gentle, and loving spirit to my children and others that both of these women gave directly to me.

My Great, Great, Grandmother: Lydia Stephens

If I wanted to learn as much as I could about my great, great, great, grandfather, I realized that the best way to do it was to learn as much as I could about his children. I know he was dedicated to his family and instilled so much of himself and of family values in them. There was only one generation removed from him and my great, great, grandmother, who is the woman I came to love and respect with all my heart.

This was the most difficult piece of my family history to understand and get to know. I am blessed to have known my great, great, grandmother through her granddaughter my great, Aunt Alma. She had a good recollection when I visited her in her New York apartment. Through her stories, I discovered my great, great, grandmother, Lydia Stephens and a lot more about my great, great, great, grandfather Titus. This was a blessing because Lydia's life was an extension of her father. By 1880, the Stephen's family reputation was well established and well respected in Albany, Georgia.

The inbred instincts of the Cushite's and my great, great, grandmother Lydia was beyond reproach. Titus and Lydia had a loving and caring father-daughter relationship. This relationship defied the common belief that slaves were just not capable of being good parents.

Their relationship taught me to understand the importance of father-daughter relationships and how to be a better father. Titus's imprint of strong, positive family values clearly impressed his sons and daughters, which transferred to his daughter, my great, great grandmother Lydia Stephens. She was a wise and respected woman. I learned, during her lifetime, that she further manifested what her father was about. She never married, which is very interesting, especially being a landowner and businesswoman. This land became heir property and is now my inheritance.

My great, great, grandmother Lydia Stephens was the mother of three, Clemmie Russell Holmes (my great grandmother), Mirah and Cherry Stephens. From the information, I got from my Aunt Alma Payne, her grandmother would spend a lot of time learning the ways of the Cherokee people. According to my great aunt Alma it was a little odd and she always wondered why her grandmother had such a strong relationship with the Cherokee people in Albany.

The Cherokee people didn't have any economic or financial status in Albany in the 1880s. What did she have to gain from that relationship? Nevertheless, this relationship went further than that of a casual one. I remember looking at a photograph of my great grandmother some years ago and she didn't look like a woman of African decent. Looking at that old photograph, it was my belief she was an offspring of the Cherokee nation. To confirm that belief, I learned from my aunt that my great grandmother had half sisters that were full-blooded Cherokee.

I then realized that Cherokee, along with European blood is a part of my heritage as an African American. I then remembered the Trail of Tears in American history. That became a double whammy to my spirit.

The Trail of Tears is when thousands of Cherokee people were forced to relocate from their lands in the south, to the midwest region, in the 1830s. There was a devastating toll to pay in sickness and death among the Cherokee nation on their journey to the midwest. Though they suffered much like the Africans, it was never in God's design to harm them. Nevertheless, to others the trail of tears was not about the welfare of the Cherokee Indians, it was about land use. What was the best way to use precious land in the South? It was a time in history when agriculture and cotton were the prime interest. Agriculture and cotton was the driving force behind the trail of tears. Today, land use is a major problem in many low-income and minority communities. Land in these communities is being redistributed for highway or redevelopments projects that in many cases do not benefit the people that are being displaced. Once property is taken from low-income and minority communities, it is difficult to regain it.

The relationship my great, great grandmother had with the Cherokee people was as guarded and revered as her African heritage. My ancestors protected that relationship as if it was a fortress of gold.

This further suggests to me that Titus Stephens Sr. had a respectful relationship with J.W. Mock. Was Titus a slave until death? I don't know. I do know his daughter was not a slave. Neither history, nor family records show how freedom was given to my great, great grandmother. It does suggest a couple of things. My great, great, great grandfather may have purchased her from J.W. Mock; or my great, great grandmother was granted her freedom at birth by J. W. Mock.

Here we go again; favor given to my great, great, great, grandfather Titus. Why? J.W. Mock and Titus Stephens somehow transcended and lived ahead of their time.

Cotton Pickers

To buy property from J.W. Mock, Titus had to earn extra money from side jobs and clever, rather than clever I should say God-inspired, negotiations.

To buy the freedom of all four children was an amazing feat. This understanding leads me to believe J.W. Mock was not an evil or typical slave owner. However, the status of freedom in an enslaved environment did not make Lydia Stephens comfortable. She understood slavery took place not only with chains, but also in a person's mind; slavery can be in one's spirit. One thing we all realized being in her midst is, she was strong for all of us. And through her actions she taught us to have that strength. Lydia's father, Titus deeded the 100 acres of land he acquired to her. This placed Lydia Stephens in a position of wealth, because she had the distinct honor of being the owner of land that had been past down to her.

There were always threats of landowners losing their land, particularly if they were Black. My Lydia understood that threat. She had to use all her wits and apply all the entrepreneurial skills she learned from her father. I can only imagine the level of stress and fear she experienced in those days from both sides of the tracks. The stress she had to deal with ranged from family members getting the land in debt to whites wanting to take the land, by any means necessary.

There were times family members borrowed from the country store, using the land as collateral. White storeowners would allow Blacks to get anything on credit and then allow that credit to get to an enormous amount, in hopes that they might collect the property one day. This had been the practice throughout the south. There was no end to what whites would do to take land from blacks.

A good example of this is when a cousin who owned 50 acres of land, near our land had gone to a general store owner and opened a tab in his store. His tab got up to $250. Once the storeowner realized he couldn't pay the $250, he told my cousin he faced beating, death, or prison, if he did not pay the bill. There was another option "his land" the 50 acres. My cousin took the lateral option signed the document and gave the store manager the 50 acres to settle the $250 debt.

In doing further research I read about the South Carolina cotton farmer named Anthony Crawford who was lynched, because he didn't accept the price a white gin owner offered for his cottonseeds. The court of law was strongly on the side of whites. They made it so that Negroes would come and go. The land stayed. In 1890's, the lynching of Negroes was a daily practice, so justice was never served. The stories go on and on. Interestingly, property was almost always involved.

The tactics of hate, terror and fear used to steal blacks land is well documented. The strategies whites used were cruel and brutal tactics. They were inhumane. Lydia, on the other hand, learned from all the lessons she was exposed to and was therefore careful in her business dealings with everybody. The Lord and the spirit of her ancestors watched over her and blessed her, as they did her father.

Another reason I think Lydia was successful in keeping her land was she was not trying to be accepted by whites. She was not about trying to live in accordance to their worldview. She was about survival and giving her family the love they need to survive.

We learned under her tutelage to stay on our guard and not allow status or wealth to make you comfortable. Living a comfortable life does not create change, and life is all about change. Though there is pride in ownership, it is not about how much you own, it is about the satisfaction of owning and creating wealth for your descendants. I know from a spiritual standpoint, we don't own anything and can never own anything. The scriptures say *"The earth is the Lord's and the fullness thereof."*

This is the foundation Lydia and Titus built. The only thing we had to do was build upon that foundation. My ancestors built all our lives on that foundation that was passed down from the Cushites.

Great Great Uncle Titus Stephens, Jr.

If there was one single man that was most impacted by my great, great, great grandfather Titus Stephens Sr., that man would be his son my great, great Uncle Titus Stephens Jr. I have heard so many amazing stories about him. To put his life and legacy into perspective using only four words, I would say: faith, wisdom, patience, and education. It is said that education is the key to success and this was the key that catapulted my great, great uncle to a position of prominence. He believed that idiom but he also understood that racism was the door he had to enter through to obtain success.

My uncle Titus Stephens Jr. is a prime example of faith in God, education, and what they can do for a family. What is interesting is that in spite of the culture and time period, he was allowed to get an education. It was in 1858 in Albany, Dougherty County, when Titus Stephens Jr. was born. Even during the civil war he was getting an education. This was a time is history when there was intentional, blatant suppression of blacks in the South. As W.E.B Dubois prescribed, Black people must be educated in order to gain a prominent status in America.

It would be untrue for me to say that whites were not a part of my rich history and that they did not play an important role in making my family's life. But, the question is still, what gave him, or, who gave him the opportunity to learn to read and write? Was it the kindness and the loving spirit of whites? Who took him in and taught him to read and write? Like my great, great, great, grandfather Titus Stephens Sr., the Lord covered him, just as Moses was covered by God from the Pharaoh who wanted to kill all males two years and under to circumvent the salvation of Israel.

It was obvious Moses could blend in with the Pharaoh and his household. While this could have been a similar case, it struck me as unbelievable (though there were some suggestions that he attended a Catholic school and, as previously mentioned, his grandfather was white). Titus Stephens Jr., the son of Titus Stephens Sr., "the slave" became a well-educated, upright man who walked with the Lord. He taught Sunday School at the little County Line Baptist Church, the same church I attended as a child. I remember walking down the dusty road about a half mile to the little County Line Baptist Church. My great grandmother Clemmie would get us up on Sunday morning and march us one by one sometimes two by two down that dusty road to church just to have Sunday school.

Where there was little known about Titus Sr., there was a lot more known about his son Titus Jr. I believe if it were not for his strong family commitments, he could have risen to great prominence and status with many other well-known black leaders of his time. Yet, he achieved greatness and the distinct honor of being the only black in east Dougherty County with a covered wagon, which would be equal to being the only person in your neighborhood to have a Learjet parked in your own hanger today.

Uncle Titus had an excitement about him. The blacks living in that part of east Dougherty County always gravitated to his house. The children would say "Let's go to Ida 'Maggie' Stephens house and get some fresh vegetables," according to my Aunt Pearle. And my great, great Uncle Titus Stephens would allow people in the community to come and get all the fresh vegetables they wanted from his beautiful garden, free of charge. His garden promoted a health-conscious community. It goes to the African American spirit of who they inherently were. If one family had food the community had food. It provided food security for those who had little or no food for their family. There was no selfishness. They shared what they had.

Today, around 15 percent of the world's food in now grown in urban areas. Gardens are in suburban areas. Agriculture is now in backyards, on roof-tops and balconies. This is good. One goal of community gardens is to create healthy communities to improve nutrition for everyone.

Life, for my ancestors, may have seemed as though it was a forgotten journey. However, that is far from truth. It was a cherished journey that continued, as they have left an indubitable impression on my family and the lives of so many others in our community.

The Bible says: *"We are as a vapor and our lives are very short".*

And during their short time on this Earth, my ancestors made their mark with every passing generation. They kept finding ways to pass on the spirit of the Cushite.

The spirit of the Cushite is the quality that contributes to society's positive growth. What drove me to write this book was I wanted to ensure the legacy of my ancestors would not be lost and forgotten. I wanted to tell their story and show how God's amazing grace allowed them to find their place in history. It is not only about land. It is about faith, growth and wealth. The rich blessings are what God and the spirit of our ancestors wish for us all.

We therefore must reach and stretch ourselves to obtain these blessings. It doesn't matter where we are or what circumstances we are in, God is there to bring us to the level of prosperity spiritually determined for each of us. In baseball, it is not a tragedy if one strikes out at bat. The tragedy is not being allowed to step up to the mound *to bat*. I believe if you just keep stepping up to the mound, sooner or later you are going to hit a ball, and it may even be a home run.

As suggested in previous chapters, there were friendly relationships between Whites and Blacks in east Dougherty County, Georgia. My Uncle Titus Jr. was one who had a unique friendship with a white man named Loke Clements. Clements was a man that believed in and wanted fairness for all, regardless of race or position. Clements would grind corn to make meal for baking and produce hams from hogs for Uncle Titus, Jr. Of course, this food was shared with the entire family: cousins, aunts, and his sisters.

One story, I was told with a humbling ending was a story that goes to the heart of Clements: It was a day like any other day. Clements went out to his barn to do some chores. There he found a Black man naked as jaybird hiding in his barn. The Black man was afraid and trembling. The reason he was naked was he had been forced to leave his house in neighboring Lee County, Georgia. He walked some 20 miles naked through the night to reach the farm of Clements.

As the story goes, the Sheriff of Lee County came to this man's house to lynch him. In a moment of panic the man ran out the back door in such a hurry, he didn't have time to put on any clothing. It was believed the sheriff was after him for a debt he owed and could not pay.

The black man had heard that Clements was a kind and fair man, who treated blacks with dignity. He asked Clements if he would help him get his property back from the sheriff. Clements told him he couldn't go up against the white sheriff in Lee County. However, if he would go back to Lee County and get his family then he would help him establish a life for his family, in east Dougherty County.

Ultimately, the man did lose his land but he was successful in getting his family to Dougherty County. I think this is an example of the way some whites made an attempt to treat blacks with dignity and respect, at that time. It is also said that Clements made sure many Blacks didn't lose their land from the evil men, who took advantage of Blacks in desperate situations.

Uncle Titus, Jr.'s time on this earth was long. Uncle Titus Jr. had lived through the great depression. He knew what it was like and didn't want his family to go through anything like that again. So, he went to Clements and made him promise not to let his family starve after his death. Once again, Titus Jr. made sure his family was safe.

Uncle Titus Stephens was around 95 years old at the time of his death in 1949. There is no clue as to what happened to him. He wandered away from home one day and was never found. Because of him the family never lacked food to eat, a home to live in or enough love to spread around.

Community Folks, Relatives

My Great Grandmother: Clemmie Russell Holmes

My family history reveals uniquely close and well-knit relationships. Around 1912, some forty-seven years after the civil war, my great grandmother Clemmie found herself in a complex situation. She had been abandoned by her husband, Benny Russell, and forced to raise her three daughters alone. This left her with limited survival options, which were to plow the fields or harvest the crops, jobs men usually perform. Relatives living nearby pitched in and helped when possible. Farming on our land became a community effort.

Clemmie Russell had respect from everybody, including white and black folks. Regardless of who you were, she could touch your life. The family thought of her as a prophetess and a lady of immeasurable wisdom. She would often have private talks with me. I am sure she did the same with all of the family, from time to time.

She spent most of her time in the woods. It was her time to meditate, time to be in her own world and spend time with the Lord. While in the woods she would often watch the guinea hens and see where they would lay their eggs. There was a great chance the eggs would be destroyed by wild dogs, snakes, or trampled by large animals. Watching the hens' movements would help her find the nest before anything happened to them. The same patience was shown toward her family. This is her legacy: a patient teacher whose classroom was the world.

In 1913, Clemmie married a stable man named Mr. Homer Holmes. Of course we all received him warmly. He was the man I know as great grandfather. Shortly afterwards, the two relocated to his home and farm in Gin Town, Georgia, which was about two miles from our home site. Later, two of my great grandmother's nephews, J.C. Garner and Acy White, who were in need of employment opportunities happened to come along at the right time to help out on the farm. That arrangement worked out well for everybody.

As the story goes, somehow my great grandfather Homer's deed to his house, which was situated on the Slappey Plantation (my mother, and Aunt Dorothy Russell's birthplace) was stolen from a family member; and sold, by an unknown source.

Years later, Homer and Clemmie moved back to her house, our home site, on County Line Road. The two nephews were left to live on the old farm site with their wives, whom they met on the plantation.

My great grandmother Clemmie Russell Holmes

My Grandparents,
Rubye and Shelby Sullivan

The survival of my ancestors is attributed to their love for family and respect for one another. At the time my great grandparents left the Slappey Plantation, my grandmother Rubye met and married my grandfather Shelby Sullivan. They moved to Eugene Clark's plantation and worked together as sharecroppers.

My mother once shared a memory with me that exemplified how blacks were treated during that time.

One day, she and a sibling were picking up pecans like they usually do, when Mary Clark came along with candy. She called them all over and told them to stand by the window. She then began deliberately dropping the candy on the ground, which they picked up and ate.

That memory, along with my grandmother telling us about all the cleaning she had to do at the Clark's house are permanently etched along the trail of my family's journey from slavery to freedom. Often, my grandmother would have to wash and iron the Clark's clothes, using lye soap, by hand.

My grandparents gave birth to my aunts and uncles on the Clark's plantation. My Aunt Pearlie was born two miles north of the George Northern railroad tracks; my Uncle Shelby Jr. was born south of those railroad tracks. My Uncle Connis was born south of Moultrie road. And my mother Virginia and Aunt Dorothy were both born north of the Moultrie road, about one mile from Spring Flats road. All the birthing places were on the Clark's plantation.

It is not clear if Homer passed away before or after the family moved off the plantation to the County Line road, but my mother recalled her mother saying how he loved his stepdaughter Dorothy. On his deathbed, he said, they had better be good to Dorothy, or else he would come back for her.

After Homer passed away, my Aunt Dorothy, Alma and great grandmother took charge of the family farm. They did business with men like Dave Gortatowsky and George Faulkner, two prominent white men, who owned trading posts (hardware stores) in Albany.

My Grandfather Shelby built a little house on the north side near my great grandmother who lived just down the road. After building his house, my grandfather had some personal challenges, so he asked two of his brothers, Arthur and Willie D., to move in.

During this time, all my family was together. One interesting problem that posed was that my great grandmother and grandmother just had too many nicknames. My great Aunt Dorothy and my mother

Virginia called my great grandmother Mama, Mama. Everyone else called her Two-Mama. My Aunt Pearlie, and Uncles Shelby Jr. and Connis, called my grandmother, Ma-ma. Later, they came up with Little Ma.

At Two-Mama's (my Great Grandmother Clemmie) house, there was an outhouse, smokehouse and chicken house. The outhouse door was an old crocked sack. That was just like the one my mother used to put her picked cotton. In the house, the only source of light was kerosene lamps. The adults stayed busy with their jobs and chores. They kept the yards and the houses clean, and would sometimes have the children help them search for chicken eggs under the house.

My grandfather organized the farming of great grandmother's land and other farms in the area as well. It was always on Good Friday that he began the planting season. When the first crop came up everyone would hoe weeds and chop the cotton, as a family. My great grandmother would come everyday to my grandmother's house. Later, she and several of the grandchildren would go back to her house at night to sleep.

August was cotton-pickin' time. They would also shake peanuts, pull corn, and pick velvet beans. (It was believed that if they fed this bean to the cows, it would produce rich milk and more delicious butter.) It was during this time period in the early 50s when farming in the south shifted from a labor to a capital-intensive enterprise. Farming was becoming more competitive and good laborers were hard to find.

After a period of time, my grandfather began to work two jobs doing his farming, during the day and public work at night. My mother and her siblings went to school during the day and worked on the farm afterwards. My great, grandmother Clemmie was certain her grand children would have good lives with a good education. All the children walked together to school everyday. The first school they attended was Porter's Corner. It was about four miles east. The second was Plummer's School. It was an additional one and a half miles west of Porter's Corner school.

When the children were older and started high school, everyone walked two and a half miles north to Acree, Georgia to catch the trailways bus to Albany. Once in Albany, they had another six or seven blocks to walk to school. Even then, before leaving for school, they had to milk the cows and tie them down. And when they came home, they had to get the cows, water them, and then let them graze.

On weekends, everyone had chores that were left over from weekdays. They swept yards, scrubbed floors and ironed. They used the older metal iron that had to be place on the stove to get it hot. They also had to cut wood for the week, especially in the winter months. And, sometimes they had to haul water for the cows to drink, or take them down to the place where they did their washing. Sundays they walked to church and had to be back before dusk.

Years later, my grandfather decided to hire out the farm and went to work for the Georgia Northern railroad. One Wednesday morning, a group of workers was working on the railroad track. They got a warning that a train was coming. My grandfather was operating a large jack and attempted to get the box cart off the track when the jack slipped. His hand got caught between the box cart and the jack. He was rushed to Phoebe Hospital in Albany, where they amputated the two fingers on his right hand. He suffered greatly and was never the same again.

With my grandfather handicapped, he felt he was half the man he used to be. He began to work odd jobs. Eventually, my grandfather left Dougherty County and moved to Moultrie Georgia, then on to Jacksonville, Florida. I remember as a child, my grandmother took me to Jacksonville, on the train to visit him. That train ride was remarkable, because it was my first experience being segregated on a train.

Years later my grandfather moved back to Albany and tried farming again, but he couldn't do it with half a hand. Not long after that he passed away. The year was 1959. That was a tremendous blow to the family. But my great grandmother and grandmother picked up the pieces and did what two aging ladies could do-- plant their gardens.

Somehow, I never could see myself leaving Georgia. It was the spirit of the place that held me. Or it may just be my desire to stay close to the two women that meant so much to me throughout my entire life. It is that same spirit that held my family together throughout the years. We are truly blessed.

We had another reminder that no matter how much we love, family separation is inevitable, whether it's through distance or death. After a long period of being bedridden, the saddest day came when our beloved Two-Mama passed away in 1979.

Field Work

We didn't realize it at the time but my Aunt Dorothy was also sick. It was a secret she kept for a long time. She and my grandmother decided to visit my Aunt Alma in New York. While there, my Aunt Dorothy. My grandmother came back to Albany alone. Not long afterward, my grandmother began suffering from the same illness as her mother. She began losing her memory due to Alzheimer. Her memory worsened as the years went on.

A day in the field

Hog killing time!

The Other Side

I would be remiss if I did not dedicate a portion of this book to my other side, my daddy's mama, Essa Mae Burrell. My father was born August 10, 1928. Essa Mae, who I also called grandma was a hard-working, defiant woman, who lived a full live in testament to her strength.

My father told me stories of how she plowed the field, driving a mule and carrying him on her back when he was a year old. When the work was hard and the sun too hot, she would place my father at the very end of the row while she plowed. She checked on him when she plowed back to the end. This is what many women had to do to hold on to a job and take care of their children at the same time.

When I was growing up I did not understand why we did not spend more time with my father's side of the family. Looking back, I see clearly how my grandma did her part in the development of the Barlow family's strength and character. She had my father out of wedlock, which made life hard for her.

Though my father's father was not married at the time of conception, he married another woman soon after Essa became pregnant. The interesting twist is she worked for him in the cotton fields. Apparently there was money owed and my grandma agreed to help pay the loan for the property. Somehow a romance flourished. After the loan was paid, she moved to town and worked in a drycleaners, until her retirement.

I remember her living in the same apartment, until she could not live alone anymore. My father brought her to live with his family. My beloved grandmother Essa Mae did well. She lived to be 94 years old and passed away July 1, 2001.

My father recollected as a teenager that all he wanted was a car. He remembered going to church and listening to the preacher talk about the power of prayer. He prayed and asked the Lord to help him somehow win a car. Well, time went along and father got frustrated thinking the Lord was not going to help him win a car. So he decided to go to work to raise the money to buy the car using the sweat of his brow. He eventually did raise enough money to purchase the car. What he learned was, a man needs to dream big and pray long, but he must put feet under the prayers for his dreams to be realized.

Can the Lord be credited for giving my father the car? The Lord gave my father the ability to work hard and buy the car. My father took advantage of the opportunity and made his God given abilities work in his favor.

My great grandfather on my father's side was also an interesting man. He held significant influence through out the entire community. His influence was needed when my great uncle Sun Barlow tragically killed a white man in the late 1930s.

From what I was told, my great uncle Sun was in a store in Albany. When the storeowner told him he owed money. My great uncle disputed the debt and walked away. The white man felt he couldn't allow a black man to "disrespect" him by walking away. So, he followed uncle Sun down the street hollering at him and screaming racial slurs.

My great uncle refused to be humiliated. He turned around reached his hand in is pocket pulled out his knife and slit the white man's throat.

By the time my uncle Sun got home, he realized he needed to hide out. He hid on his father my great grandfather, Peter Barlow's farm. Of course, that was the first place the sheriff looked. Sure enough, the sheriff came and asked my great grandfather if Sun was there. My grandfather told the sheriff, "no." He lied. The sheriff took my great grandfather at his word and left.

Can you imagine the uproar in Albany, Georgia over a black man killing a white man in the late 30s? If caught he most certainly would have been lynched. However, he was caught and he eventually went to trial. He was found guilty on a lesser charge and served

5 years in prison. After serving his time in prison, he returned home to Albany.

Yet, in the minds of many whites, justice was not done. They still wanted to lynch him. After months of the family trying to convince Uncle Sun, he should leave Albany, he finally agreed it was best for him and the family. He moved to Jacksonville, Florida where he lived out the remainder of his life. He died of natural causes.

The Early Years: An Age of Destruction and Determination

As I look back on my early years, I remember being taught to feel optimistic about life in spite of all the negative images portrayed in the media and everywhere else. We were continuously reminded of the fact that we are "covered by the blood." My grandfather died in 1959, my mother was separated from my father. During most of my childhood there was no male figure in the household to teach the manly responsibilities in life.

However, there were these wonderful women, who not only taught us important values and principles, they taught us to have self-respect and respect for others. I defy anyone today who attempts to tell me who I am. Or to try to define me other than the man I know myself to be, a strong African from the Cushite tradition born in America and covered by the blood of Jesus Christ.

The spiritual force around me has always challenged me to ask the critical questions about the impact of segregation, integration, and Jim Crow laws, during the 50s and 60s. There are some people who, no matter how the world looks upon them, they have an overarching aura of pride that sustains them. They know how to give respect; and, they know how to receive respect from others. Such a person was my great grandmother Clemmie, the eagle of our family. She and others watched over us and protected us from the horrors of the South.

I will never forget the times white boys my age would call my grandmother "Rubye." I did not like the blatant and deliberate disrespect they showed her. So one day, I told my grandmother I was going to call one of their mothers or grandmothers by the first name, just to show them how it feels. My grandmother was firm when she said to me, "Young man, you had better not call any grown up simply by their first name. You will be a respectful young man, regardless of what others do, or say."

I grew up very well aware of the imbalance and injustice among the races. I hated the fact that white people got away with demanding respect from black people and did not give respect in return. At the time, I thought my great grandmother was afraid of the consequences. I later realized that it would not have been a wise thing for me to do. We were taught to be the bigger person and to take the high road in life.

Throughout the early 1950s, my family's future felt uncertain to me. In spite of that I was instructed to go to school and focus on my studies and not to worry about the livelihood of the family. Many children at that time were compromising their education, working the fields, picking and chopping cotton to help support their families. For us, education was seen as a priority.

The youth of those days did not have jobs at fast food places after school. It was all about agriculture. That was the number one industry and the only option made available to young black children, outside of household chores. According to statistics and economic indicators, we were considered "clinically" poor but we were so rich in love that it became the life support that sustained us and gave us a reason to breathe.

I didn't recognize anxiety or the fear of survival in the faces of my family. If there was ever an occasion to witness first-hand the strength of a woman, it was during this vulnerable time in American history.

I can never forget the nightriders (the veiled members of the Klu Klux Klan) these were bankers, lawyers, farmers, businessmen and politicians by day and terrorists by night. Their agenda, simply stated, was to terrorize and intimidate the "Niggers AKA Blacks AKA Africans." Their methods were atrocious and designed to keep blacks uneducated and disenfranchised. I recall one of them coming to our house. It was a day or so before my grandfather's funeral. I stood near my grandmother listening, as if I placed myself there to protect. I was eight or nine and this was during the time when children were not allowed to be present when adults were talking. But I remember. He never properly greeted my grandmother.

There wasn't a knock on the door. He just came on the porch and called my grandmother outside. He said, "Rubye, I will buy this land and you can live in this house and stay on, as long as you want." My grandmother listened to him as he spoke. He proposed to give her a few thousand dollars and we would work for him. This is the white man, whose house my grandmother cleaned. His plan was to have us sharecrop and work for little or nothing on what he hoped would become his farm.

Of course, I had little voice in family matters. But I, along with my siblings, wanted to do everything possible to keep our family going and growing with dignity. My great grandmother always said, "If a white man comes and offers you one thousand dollars for our land, it must be worth a whole lot more." Come hell, or high waters, we were determined to hold on to the land. It was not that the white man needed the land. He felt entitlement. And he didn't want to see my family with it. On the eve of grandfather's funeral he wanted to buy our inheritance, our freedom, our sense of pride and destroy our future generations.

But none of it was for sale!

She didn't imply anything on that day. However, she knew the answer before he stepped off the porch. That would have been tantamount to us selling our souls to the devil.

My Family, Post-Slavery Years

One way to understand even more about my ancestors is to know and understand the conditions of life in the mid 1800s.

Cotton was king.

I can only imagine how difficult it must have been to be a slave and a Christian at the same time. We are taught to love our enemies, which included slave masters as well. I often ponder what gave them the amazing strength to move beyond slavery and become landowners and entrepreneurs. How did they get the strength and courage to elevate from being property to owning property? It had to be a trust in God and his ability to entrust knowledge in those it would affect the most.

So many times life's unfairness will put us in places and situations that cause us to think of ourselves as victims. However, we don't have to let any past circumstance dictate our future. I believe it is choice, not chance that determines one's destiny.

Similar circumstances such as this occur in the Bible as it pertains to Joseph. He was sold into slavery, to an African from Egypt, by his brother and later resold to the Pharaoh. Eventually, he ended up in prison. This is an example of a Cushite man, favored by God who was delivered from his persecutors to gain great social and political status in Egypt. The whole scene took place in Africa.

Joseph became prime minister and succeeded in having his father Jacob and all his brothers brought there to live under his authority. The scripture tells us that in Israel's dying hours, he took Joseph's two sons Manasseh and Ephraim, the sons of an Egyptian woman, and blessed them. It was the Egyptian woman's sons that inherited the promise of God with passing of the patriarchal heritage.

Just as God allowed Joseph's sons to inherit blessing from Joseph, he allow my great, great, great grandfather to pass on his heritage to his sons and daughters. It is apparent that neither race, nor color should be any indicator of success. My point is, God has not given us a spirit of fear, but a spirit love, and of a sound mind.

It is said, "Adversity breeds strength, but not for the weak hearted." Remember the biblical story of David. He had great faith in Israel and he depended on God's grace. According to I Samuel 16:1, Goliath stood over 12 feet tall. As Goliath began to talk, all the men of Israel fled from him in fear. Israel experienced stress, fear, worry, hopelessness, despair, discouragement, depression, and a sense of defeat. However, David, who was small in stature stood like a giant, strong and tall, with God at his side. And we all know how the story ended.

The huge lesson here is, as long as you know the Lord is with you, any enemy is defeated regardless of color. I must also say, God does not like lazy people. He understands wandering sheep (people). That is the nature of people. But lazy, disobedient people are not pleasing to him. And they will never be successful. We must continually fight the good fight of faith.

We are connected to God. "Be sober; be vigilant because your adversary the devil walks about seeking people he may devour. (I Peter 5: 8-9). Our enemy is stress, fear, worry, hopelessness, despair, discouragement, and depression. It all manifests itself as self-doubt and ultimately self-defeat.

Today, as I walk the land my great, great, great grandfather owned, I feel the spirit of Titus Stephens Sr. This spiritual connection gives me strength and courage to face life's challenges, knowing whatever the situation I am in, I will be lead by God.

For a long time I struggled to understand why black people have the issues we have, the "Black lack." And what is it that prevents us, as a community, from creating a solution.

I became a member of an organization called Restoration 2000. This is an organization of Black men in Albany, Georgia that meet regularly to develop methods to restore African American men to a place of dignity. This aided me in my efforts to realize that we have great minds. And, we are a people of courage, strength, and tenacity.

We can and do rise to the Cushite standard. This is the thing that propels me. I cannot rest. We cannot rest. I do not give up. We should never give up. I shall strive to be better. We should strive to be a better community and not be satisfied with unsatisfactory conditions in which we may find ourselves.

We must continue to teach our children to never settle for anything less than their absolute best. We should also emphasize that life is great when you are about life-long learning. We should never stop growing…

Invisible Slave Owners

During the early to mid 1900s a great mass of the black population in Dougherty County worked the land, paying for rent and all of their physical needs through a crop-sharing system.

To explain the sharecropping system: the landowner enters into contract (mostly unwritten) with an individual, or family, to farm his land in exchange for a percentage in share of the profits gained from farming operations. In many cases, the sharecropper rents living space from the landowner. For example, let's say the cotton crop product is $1,000 that year. The landowner could receive up to two-thirds of that $1,000, which would be $750. This leaves the sharecropper with very little money to pay rent and to live on for that year. In the worst-case scenario, if cotton prices were high the landowner would raise the rent for that year leaving the sharecropper with approximately the same amount of money as if the price were low. This is not far removed from slavery.

My grandmother and grandfather on my mother's side were a part of this system in Dougherty County at the beginning of their marriage. They worked on the Clark's plantation for a few years. My aunts, uncles, and mother were born in different houses all over the Clark's plantation. It was not what my grandfather Titus Sr. envisioned for his family. They were not progressing in terms of economic freedom.

I don't think it was my grandmother's decision to sharecrop. It was a decision of my grandfather made, thinking it would be beneficial for his family. My grandmother was following her husband. It was my great grandmother Clemmie, who convinced my grandfather to move off the Clark's plantation to work on the family farm. They were on the verge of falling into an endless cycle that so many blacks in Dougherty County fell into, which ultimately would have ended in debt.

In Dougherty County, in the early to mid 1900s, Blacks acquired huge amounts of land. If blacks today would have held onto their land, or left it in the hands of other Blacks, Blacks would own today nearly thirty thousand acres in Dougherty County.

Thank God again for the Cushite spirit in Titus Sr. He knew as an enslaved man that the only way to acquire real freedom was to own your land and produce for yourself. And Clemmie reminded them of that.

In 1898 the land holdings in Albany, Georgia were as follows:

- Under forty acres belonged to forty-nine families;

- Forty to two-hundred and fifty acres belonged to seventeen families;

- Two-hundred and fifty to one thousand acres belonged to thirteen families;

- One thousand or more acres belonged to two families.

The key to keeping Blacks out of the American mainstream of wealth was to keep them in debt. My forefathers understood that debt was the inability to make income cover expenses. Ultimately, debt is an invisible slaver and the owner of your debt is your enslaver. We would do well to understand that basic rule today.

Lessons Learned

The spirit of the Cushites of modern times continues through men like "my great, great, great grandfather," who loved his family and taught his children to continue to grow and never let the enemy get into their heads. That they should work to reunite and reestablish rightful positions and birthrights to land both in America and Africa.

As a child, I remember my brothers, sisters and cousins and I would always find time for laughter. We were happy playing games like hop scotch, hide and seek, Simon Says, marbles, or spinning tops, dancing, telling jokes and just running up and down the road. We had fun. I think we were reminding ourselves that we are human and that no one has the authority to deprive us of our joy, despite the things we didn't have. It was our way of telling the world we are proud people and we are restoring our dignity to that of the Cushites.

Sometimes, I think of the message it also sent to white people, who would watch us work day-in and day-out. But we were still happy. They would say, sometimes out loud, "Those lil niggers are fine with things just the way they are." That was far from the truth. What did the Cushites do when they had to smile in a situation that was horrible? They let go and let God bless them. The Lord covered the Cushites with his blood. Their spiritual connection from the Lord bestowed upon them a plan to be prophets and to remain unharmed.

I am writing this book to honor my ancestors. I am very proud of the heritage she and the others passed on to my family. That heritage is not only educational, but that has spiritually gotten us to where we are today, with the right to gaining an education and obtaining wealth. Yes, even wealth. I will always appreciate and cherish their vision of wealth.

"Those who profess to favor freedom and deprecate agitation, are men who want crops without plowing up the ground; they want rain with thunder and lightning."

- Frederick Douglass, 1857

I do my best by learning what I can and taking advantage of opportunities that come my way. I teach my sons and daughters the same. As intriguing as Titus' life was, I often wonder what it would be like to transplant my life into his situation. Then, I think about Lydia Stephen seeing her son sold on the auction block in Charleston, South Carolina. I pray that the Lord comforted her and gave her peace, during that lonely and depressing time in her life.

My struggles gave me answers to many difficult questions I grew up with in the South. I wondered why

I had to sit in the back of the bus, why there were two separate water fountains, why I had to go to the back door of white peoples' houses. Why do black people in this country have so many issues? What happened to us? When did it happen? And why? These are questions that many of us are still trying to answer.

Looking at the obvious pathology of our young men and women the sagging pants, loud music, profane vocabulary, disrespect for themselves and others. The remedy is not clear at all. Who did we lose ourselves to? And, who is benefiting from this self-deprecating behavior?

This not-so "silent killer" poisons our minds, hearts and spirits. It wreaks havoc on our families for generations. Looking closer, this maze of confusion was put together one piece at a time: day by day, week by week, year by year.

In spite of positive influences like that of many of our forefathers, there is an evil spirit that still prevails throughout the South. A friend of mine told me a story about his grandson, who wished he was white, so he could own a store and live in a big white house. This story is sad and one that I will never forget.

My question is, why does this spirit, this energy, still persist? Society taught this child and many others that he had to be white to have the things that come with success and privilege. Even as a child this young man had a heightened awareness of "white privilege" and "black lack."

However, the grace of God does not lead us into darkness just to leave us there. It brings us through the darkness in order to see the light. The maze of confusion began to make sense when I asked the difficult questions. I believe we stop functioning or growing when we stop questioning ourselves about the things that surround us. No one, except God, can degrade the soul within each of us.

"The soul that is within me no man can degrade."

Frederick Douglass

The Old House

It was a rickety, old house that kept us from the elements in the winter, summer, spring, and fall. It was strong yet weak. Looking back on the house that I called home for all my childhood life, it was a remarkable house that played a critical part in teaching me about life. The house was old in the 50's. It was built in the late 1800's by my great, great, uncle Titus Stephens Jr. The house sat off the road about one eight of a mile and was made completely of wood, with a tin roof. The only brick on the house was the chimney.

We were so embarrassed to have guests and were ashamed to let anyone know this was the house we lived in. The goal was to avoid, at all cost, someone discovering this was our house. It was shameful to us for the school bus to drive us to the doorsteps or to have some nice person bring us home after school. Added to the pressure of growing up in the south with segregation and the evil systems thereof, this old house was an added pressure we all assumed on ourselves.

Yet this house kept us safe. It stood through the strong winds and storms. It stood tall and proud as to say to itself "I am a proud house. I have stood for decades and have not fallen. I have sheltered many in my days even though I am old and my wood is wrinkled. I am old and the tin on my roof is old and rusty and sometime has to be nailed back after a bad storm, I am still strong and proud."

When it rained, we would have to put several pots on the floor to catch the rain. There were weak boards on the floor and steps. Many times we would remind each other where the weak spot was. We would hate to see an overweight person come to visit, because we knew that meant they might find the weak spot in the floor and fall through it. It was always a tough job to find the board to replace the broken one, not to mention the potential embarrassment. Yet, there was no doubt this house was built strong and made out of the best of material. It just had a few weak spots. It was like everything else that has weaknesses.

In reality, this house was a teacher. From this old house, we can all learn a lesson or two. Our house was not always weak. It was built around the turn of the century and made of very good material. Not one time did we have to rebuild any portion of the house after a storm. The wind blew and the house stood. It had a solid foundation. It reminds me of my great, great, great grandfather, of two-mama, Aunt Dorothy and my grandmother Rubye (little mama). They were made of good material and protected us just like that old house. And, there were times when we, as children, reacted towards them the same way we did the old house. They were old, born around the turn of the century. They did not wear the latest apparel. They wore what they had and did not try to impress others.

We did not want them to come to school for fear of others seeing how old they were. My grandmother came one day to check on me. She wanted to see if I was safe after someone took a message to her saying I had gotten hurt and was in serious condition. She traveled several miles from the country into town, just to check on me. The principal called me to the office and there was my great grandmother standing there. I was ashamed and embarrassed to see her standing there in her old dress, with her apron sagging about the waist.

It took until I became an adult to understand why they were so proud. She was strong and was made of the good stuff. She had a solid foundation. And just like that old house, she stood strong for decades and we have learned from her wisdom. Now, I am ashamed to think that there was ever a time in my life when I was embarrassed to see her. She always loved and protected us. And, like that old house she taught us that no matter how young we are, one day you will get old.

The winds of life will beat upon you. What seem to be never-ending are the rainfalls in your life. And, in time, your body will get weakened. You will begin to break down at some point. There well be times when people (probably your children) will laugh at you and be ashamed of you and not appreciate what you do or what you have done, for them and others. But, there will come a time when they will miss that, like the old saying describes. "You don't miss your water until the well runs dry." I thank the old house for watching over me, even when I was I ashamed to call it my home. I thank my grandparents for loving me and being there even when I was stupid.

I am so proud of that old house and thankful it kept us. The house was not blown down by the winds. It never did fall down. We did tear the old house down in 1970, partially out of shame, after we built our new house, I am ashamed to say.

Racism Forever?

To understand the success of my ancestors is to understand the social contract of the American South. This is a contract that was not written, nor spoken in mixed company. It is a contract that was hidden, one that blacks could neither see nor feel and that required an understanding of it if they were to beat the odds for blacks' success, in America.

Do you know what it is, or how the social contact works? If not, I will explain. The social contract is drawn up by the proverbial lines in the sand. They are inferred social, physical, and mental boundaries. The contract stipulates endless dos and don'ts for blacks' behavior when relating to whites, ways to bow and not make eye contact, which was a social practice in the Deep South and many parts of Africa. It was a social tool used to maintain social divide. And when fully implemented is institutional racism, at best.

This is one of the reasons why Africans in Africa, through colonization, and Africans in America, through slavery, had their "place in society."

Growing up in the Deep South meant adhering to this social contract and learning the lessons that were essential for survival. These lessons were passed down from generation to generation and are as old as the institution of slavery in America. Years were spent learning and perfecting these lessons. They are effective.

The Word of God says "...There is a time to keep silent and a time to speak." Who knew that this was the one rule blacks in the South would learn and incorporate into their survival strategy? Some referred to it as a "code of silence," and as usual, this code benefited whites more than blacks. It sounds like something the CIA might employ.

Today, while it is perfectly acceptable for a black person to talk to a white person about something another black person said or did, it was never acceptable for blacks to talk to whites about what a white person said or did in the Deep South. White people, no matter how rich or poor, were not to be talked about by blacks. That went hand-in-hand with the notion that whites could do no wrong. And, if they did, you only heard talk about it. Rarely would anything happen to them.

The only bad things we heard about white people were things blacks did to them. Whites were always considered perfect and genteel, incapable of committing violent crimes. That is the perception whites wanted us to have, in spite of the horrific lynchings going on all around us. After all, white men were the ones made in the image of God. And the Black man was not At least, that is what the white depictions of Jesus the Christ reveals.

To go deeper in the understanding of this, you have to understand the political and social culture of the South. Big cities like Atlanta might have been more enlightened, but in smaller cities and towns, the code was the rule.

Nowadays people can contrast that back-story with recent history. Remember the Waco siege in Texas 1993? That slaughter ultimately resulted in the deaths of four FBI agents and more than eighty members of the Branch Dravidian sect. Then there was the high school massacre, in Columbine, Colorado in 1999, by Eric Harris and Dylan Klebold, where two white teens shot and killed a dozen students, a teacher, and wounded 23 others before killing themselves.

There are several events along this scale that left everyone talking about what we must do as humans to make sense of it all and fix the problem. Blacks and whites were finally able to talk to one another about crimes not restricted to race or zip code.

I remember my first few months in college and how excited I was to be there. It was a small private college in Thomasville, Georgia. Did I say this was a major deal for me? It was beyond exciting for a young black man from a small black high school to attend this college.

It was there that I found my first white instructor. Thank God, he was a nice and fair person. I found him easy to talk to. That was important, since I was the only black student in his class. He was from Philadelphia and taught college part time, while working on his doctorate degree at Florida State University.

One day, he invited the class to lunch at McDonald's. We ordered our meals and they went to sit down to eat. I went to a different part of the restaurant to eat alone. The professor came looking for me. Of course, he found me eating at a table by myself and wanted to know why I was not eating with the rest of the class. He never got the answer, because I didn't offer him one. I was simply doing what I had been taught all my life: blacks didn't eat, nor talk with whites in public places.

He, being from Philadelphia, didn't have a clue about the unspoken rules, the "code" of the Deep South. It was, however, a time of sadness for me. Here it was, a hundred and twenty-five years post-emancipation and twenty years after the 1964 Civil Rights Act passed, and I found myself exhibiting signs of mental enslavement. How could this happen to me?

It took my white professor to remind me that I was not a slave. I knew that. It was clear, in spite of all my good home training, and Cushite legacy. I hadn't made the choice to fully embrace it. I was unable to get past the segregated bathrooms, lunch counters, nightriders and the riding at the back of the bus. I was unable to get past the code.

It was that day when I realized how tightly this powerful mental constraint can hold even the strongest ones. I was set free that day and began to practice what

about. It's one thing to be a slave and another to act like one. Just like my great, great, great grandfather taught his children and his children taught their children the stories contained in this book, this is my attempt to teach my children to not act as though they are enslaved.

There is so much to offer this world and an enslaved mind is not characteristic of the Cushites.

If there is one thing I learned, it would be that we accept what we want to accept. No matter what situation you may find yourself in, there is a way out if you listen to the Word. The Lord has not forgotten you. And neither have your ancestors.

This is the assurance handed down from my great, great, great, great grandmother Lydia; to my great, great, great grandfather Titus Stephens Sr.; to his daughter my great, great, grandmother Lydia Stephens and his son, my great, great Uncle Titus Stephens Jr.; to my great grandmother Clemmie Holmes (the daughter of Lydia Stephens); to my grandmother Rubye Sullivan; and her daughter Virginia Seabrook, my mother; and to me. My entire family rests in that assurance and enjoys all the things our parents taught us. And we are stronger because they lived a life of dignity.

As I walk the land that remains in my family for over one hundred and fifty years, I give thanks for the grace of our Lord and Savior Jesus Christ, for we have been "Covered by the Blood."

Thanks to everyone for all my lessons...

The Age Of Growth